This book belongs to:

_____

_____

_____

First published by Walker Books Ltd.
87 Vauxhall Walk, London SE11 5HJ

Copyright © 1999 by Lucy Cousins
Lucy Cousins font copyright © 1999 by Lucy Cousins

Based on the audio visual series "Maisy." A King Rollo Films production for
Universal Pictures International Visual Programming. Original script by Jeanne Willis.

Maisy™. Maisy is a registered trademark of Walker Books Ltd., London.

First U.S. edition 1999

Library of Congress Cataloging-in-Publication Data

Cousins, Lucy.
Maisy dresses up / Lucy Cousins.—1st U.S. ed.
p. cm.
Summary: Maisy the mouse makes a very special costume for Tallulah's costume party.
ISBN 0-7636-0885-8 (hardcover)—ISBN 0-7636-0909-9 (paperback)
[1. Costumes—Fiction. 2. Parties—Fiction. 3. Mice—Fiction.
4. Animals—Fiction.] I. Title.
PZ7.C83175Mae 1999
[E]—dc21 98-43219

8 10 9

Printed in China

This book was typeset in Lucy Cousins.
The illustrations were done in gouache.

Candlewick Press
2067 Massachusetts Avenue
Cambridge, Massachusetts 02140

visit us at www.candlewick.com

Maisy Dresses Up

Lucy Cousins

CANDLEWICK PRESS
CAMBRIDGE, MASSACHUSETTS

Maisy has been invited to Tallulah's costume party.

What will Maisy be?

She looks in her
dress-up box.

She could be
a pirate.
But Charley is
already dressed
up as a pirate.

She could be
a queen.
But Eddie is
already dressed
up as a king.

Maisy has a good idea! She will make her own special costume.

Charley, Eddie, and Cyril are already at Tallulah's house when . . .

. . . the doorbell rings.
In comes a zebra.

Oh, it's Maisy!

Hello, everyone.
It's party time!

Lucy Cousins is one of today's most acclaimed author-illustrators of children's books. Her unique titles instantly engage babies, toddlers, and preschoolers with their childlike simplicity and bright colors. And the winsome exploits of characters like Maisy reflect the adventures that young children have every day.

Lucy admits that illustration comes more easily to her than writing, which tends to work around the drawings. "I draw by heart," she says. "I think of what children would like by going back to my own childlike instincts." And what instincts! Lucy Cousins now has more than thirteen million books in print, from cloth and picture books to irresistible pull-the-tab and lift-the-flap books.